Poor folk/s.

An anthology of short stories.

Tokelo Hlagala.

Foreword

By PHUMULANI MNGOMEZULU (Award winning author).

For many years of my life, I used to mainly understand stories in terms of their milieu — what they could teach me about a particular social context and its dynamics. However, through time, as my consciousness has become more and more identified with the human spirit, I have come to appreciate stories as pathways to understanding matters of the human condition and the questions that surround it: What is the meaning of my existence? What is good? What is evil? What do I do about all my love, guilt, hate, lust, envy, fear, mourning and rage? Does anybody love me? What happens when I die? Who Am I? The literary world has helped me analyse life and my own existence more fully than anything else in my life. For as long as a story is driven by human characters, in literature I have something to learn and explore about my own humanity through these characters. As I immerse myself in the lives of these characters and what they have to deal with, whether or not these characters are from a country that I am familiar with, the gender that I am, or the culture and social dynamic that I am accustomed to, by virtue of the human dilemma, they teach me something about who I am beyond domestication. The takeaway becomes the realization and appreciation that I am not alone in these matters. I write this foreword because I have come to know Tokelo Hlagala as an earnest advocate of this very notion. This author's love and yearning for storytelling — for illuminating the human condition — is deep and sacred. That he is able to communicate his ideas about humanity and society with such sway and lucidity, is more than I can think of. Over the years we have become dear friends, occasional collaborators, and fellow travellers on this quest to illuminate the human condition through our work. I trust Tokelo's heart and I honour his keen intellect. He is a wonderful writer with a mind of his own.

Reading the stories in this anthology has been an interesting experience for me. These stories not only highlight themes that I am intimately familiar with, but the anthology also contains a couple of stories that took me to a place in my own life that involved profound moments of ignorance — where I missed opportunities to be a better human being to someone else because my lens was not calibrated. Each time I revisit these stories and see these themes expressed in new and different language, I re-experience — at deeper and deeper levels of awareness — the Beauty they contain.

In Intersections, the narrator, Thapelo is a young engineer from a village in the Northern Cape, who is fresh from college and has come to the city of Johannesburg to find work and apply his trade. However, he soon learns that life in modern South Africa is more complicated than what he had thought — he is unable to find work in the field he is educated for. Driven by the need to adapt to his circumstances and survive, he gets knocked in a completely different life. Not only does this story shine light upon the unemployment crisis in South Africa, but it is also a powerful narration about our sense of humanity — or lack of — through our daily interactions in the streets.

For Whom The Bell Tolls is a story about how poverty separates us in the Vale of Tears.

Through the life of the narrator in this story, and his experiences in his world of wanting, we learn about poverty as a nuance to how a person may age gracefully, learn to develop a sense of self-worth and belonging, cultivate their drive and ambition, and how one of the most important resources that is inherent in every human being can easily be silenced in the life of the poor person — their Voice.

How Will It Happen? is perhaps the most important story in this anthology, if you will. This story highlights two important themes for me — firstly, the issue around how patriarchal-dominant systems in the household not only dehumanize women, but also provide a practical model for young girls that the voice and opinion of a woman do not matter — that it must be frowned upon, and if a woman were ever to attempt to raise her voice and opinion, she must not speak up or speak with confidence because that is somehow undignified and disrespectful towards her husband. In this story, the author suggests that the worm at the core may primarily be through husbands who do not regard their wives with the respect and dignity that any human being deserves, and how daughters see that as a model for what good looks like for marriage and the definition of what it means to be a good wife. This brings me to the second important theme that this story highlights for me — domestic violence and abuse. Because the young girl grows up with the belief that a good wife is defined by how much disrespect and dehumanization, she is willing to take from a man, the author suggests that some cases of domestic violence and abuse may happen from such situations. In this particular instance, one could say that perhaps the onus is on the woman to confront and heal her childhood trauma before considering marriage in order to avoid such precarious situations, or the other perspective could be that the power is with the man who needs to heal his trauma and question his idea of what it means to be masculine so that he never creates the conditions for such situations to occur in the first place. In this story, Tokelo makes us think hard about these two opposing ideas.

I cannot find enough words to lucidly describe how A Day In the Life of Zandi makes me feel. It is a shockingly indescribable image that this author paints in this story to drive a painful, yet powerful message home, fitting for this anthology's end. I absolutely enjoyed reading these stories. They made me think. I hope that through these short stories, and this mighty pen of Tokelo Hlagala, you too may also experience in your own unique way, this author's beautiful exploration of the Dukkha.

With all my humanity,

Phumulani M.

Poor folk, a prayer (Hope & pray).

My breeders hoped and prayed that "nothing
happens" but I happened and affliction
began.
Frustrations, fears and feuds fuelled anxieties
and they panicked.
Like PE weather they experienced four seasons
of emotions in one day.
The thoughts of I, being a blessing kept their
hopes up.
The understanding of I, being a "mistake" kept
them up at night.
The hope that this was not true haunted their
already crippled souls.
They indeed hoped and prayed that I was a
passing-by nightmare.
I am the poor folk!
I am the poor folk!
I am the poor folk!

Mine is to hope and pray that all shall be well.
I find myself contemplating about my faith, is it
strong or made strong by circumstances.
I stop myself from trying to believe that
temporal situations are permanent.
I stumble and fumble upon my actions and

utterances.
The world has become an island, and I am
content to live on it in my broken heart
because I must deviate from humanity.
I am the poor folk!
I am the poor folk!
I am the poor folk!

Daily I hope and pray for:
A better job opportunity.
Better and different childhood ,even
adulthood.
A different environment.
Better and improved mental health.
Physical strength to carry on when the
mountain becomes steeper.
A fair and just society.

I hope and pray for a better life.
But for now, still, I remain a poor folk!

Zuko Gqadavama.

Poor Folk/s.

Short stories.

Tokelo Hlagala.

Poor Folk/s.

...Mine is to hope and pray that all shall be well.
I find myself contemplating about my faith, is it
strong or made strong by circumstances,
I stop myself from trying to believe that temporal
situations are permanent...

Intersections.

I ntersections represent points of connections and separations, the connection of two roads, the separation of two or more areas. We have a lot of these intersections. These points of connections and separations influence decisions and give rise to questions such as, do I go right, left, or continue forward at this intersection? The above is true for many at many intersections like this one I am seated nearby. To me, this intersection amongst many things represents the intersection of stories, people coming from all walks of life, fleeing something, and pursuing something. Daily, at this intersection, there are a plethora of interactions. If you look at all the men that I am seated with at this intersection, you will realize the kaleidoscope of these stories that I speak of, I akin they have my own story. The analogous theme of our stories seated here, is our pursuit for economic emancipation from the poverty and deprivation that we all come from, some from a deeper abyss of poverty than others. Some come very far to arrive at this intersection, from neighboring countries, from neighboring provinces, and a few just from around here.

This is said to be the city of gold, perhaps that is why many of us have migrated to this part of the country with its vast opportunities, but not everything is as it seems, and as said to be.

It's Monday morning. A few minutes ago, a bakkie came speeding, crossed the traffic lights when they were orange just about to transition red to stop all the cars that came in the same direction as the bakkie. A second after his front tires passed the pedestrian crossing the traffic lights turn red. He had beaten the traffic lights as he seemed to desire. He seemed to be in a rush to somewhere. The bakkie stopped just a couple of steps away from us. There was no asking or speaking that took place, all the gentlemen that were seated, some on the pavement, some on rocks and bricks, all of them picked up their bags and ran at an alarming pace towards the car. They left nothing but dust behind their footsteps.

I was part of these men who ran to the bakkie like a Jozi thief that just saw a fidelity truck tumbling and money scattering all over. This bakkie represented something akin to a fidelity truck, it represented potential temporary employment for us, sometimes permanent employment, if the goddess of luck was on your side. However, that was rare, in the two years that I have been at this corner, such a thing only occurred once, and it was hearsays. No one was ever absolute about the story of this one gentleman who was said to have received permanent employment right from this very corner.

The beauty of this hustle lies within its absence of interviews. There are no assessments that we ought to partake in, there are no references of previous employment required for our temporary employment, those are for skilled jobs, where there are key performance areas and job descriptions. Here there are no job descriptions.

Tokelo Hlagala.

Here, the only indication that you can do the job is through the work suites and boots you're wearing.

The blue work suites with a reflective stripe of yellow and boots are our curriculum vitae at this busy intersection that separates the slums from affluence, that separate conversations about stokvels and societies to those about stock markets and liquidity.

Many like I, gather here looking for employment every day of the week. Some have placards written amongst the many things– *painting, welding, gardening,* and other specialties, underlining with contact details, always cellphone numbers. At this part of the corner, there are no emails, no LinkedIn profiles, they are unknown. The fourth revolution with its advancement and niceties has no place in this corner of the world.

The new members are usually the ones you find having placards where they have written the job they want to do, but eventually, they throw them away. They realize it is one's speed that matters. They soon realize that job selection is a luxury unknown in this part of the world, they recall and realize that they left an empty refrigerator and there might be no food tomorrow, they become aware that they left kids at home who need food and wives who are looking and expecting them to provide. They soon realize that, here, there is no time for talking and motivating how much one deserves an opportunity, the most essential goal is to see yourself inside that bakkie as it releases smoke from behind and drives away to greener pastures.

'I only need three people. The rest please go back, I don't need you.' The white man had spoken without even looking at us, he had an expression of annoyance and disgust, maybe at our state of poverty, or maybe he was just having a bad morning. You let your wondering sense do its job. One can never fully comprehend human behavior, especially from those of a different background.

It was survival of the quickest at this part of the world, your running speed was the one thing that decided your fate for the day. Today I am very lucky, my feet did not stutter and disappoint me. I am part of the three gentlemen that are now in this bakkie traveling with this strange white gentleman. With the hustle that we are in, we meet different people every day, from all walks of life and backgrounds. Black people, white people, Indians. We meet young adults, our age mates who always ignite this feeling of disdain and self-loathing within us as we wonder... 'why am I not like them? Why am I not living my dream successfully? what wrongs have I committed to the universe?' They always make me wonder, but then I quickly realize that I am not alone in this storm. There are many like me not only at my corner but in a plethora of corners of the country.

I have come to believe that to a certain point we are victims of circumstances, to what extent I am not certain, the places we come from have a hand in how our lives pan out. One can be smart and hardworking, come from a place that does not allow them to flourish, the other can be fairly good in what they do, and because they come from places that allow them to flourish, they ascend to the top of the world.

Could it be that some of these successful age mates that I see come from the same place as i? if so, what could they have done to reach their success that I have failed to do? These questions molest me on many hostile days and nights.

In this hustle, we meet kindhearted people, at the same time we meet mean-mannered people, but that is not something that exists only here, it is a world phenomenon. These are characteristics that are shared by everyone across all societies regardless of class and status.

This hustle has exposed me to places that I am sure I will never afford even if I lived 10 lifetimes. The kind of places that make me feel that I was born into this world merely to accompany these men and women as they thrive in their castles.

Just last week we were collected at this very corner by a gentleman who was the driver of the house we were going to work at. Our task for that day as we found out upon arrival was to clean and remove all the waste that was left after a pool extension. We never entered that house but passing by the window I saw a portrait of a man that I presume to be the owner of the house standing with the minister of finance. There are many stories that I can

Tokelo Hlagala.

relate about some of the people that I have met through this hustle, and I know many would not believe me and my stories. After all who am I?

The two gentlemen that won the race with me today are Vusumzi (who we call Mavusi) and Thabo, commonly referred to as Sthibo. I first met Sthibo here over a year ago.
Mavusi originally comes from Kwazulu-Natal in some village whose name I have forgotten. Mavusi, like many of the gentlemen that you will find at our intersection in the early morning of the weekdays, has a story of how he landed up here. He narrated to me his story once.

    'Dyan'endala..., *he calls everyone*
Dyan'endala... You see Dyan'endalal was staying with peace, good peace
Dyan'endala, with my father and mother. The connection between me and my stepmother was not *phashasha*, but it was not bad bad, I moved from her way, she moved away from my way and my things, like my room, she did not come there. My father was married her

22

Poor Folk/s.

after he divorce my mother. My mother goes back to her mother house you see, but she say that I must stay with my father, because us Africans believe the children belong to the family of the father.

My mother did not have many problems with that, as long as I come to her mother's place to visit her sometime, plus there was no bedroom for me at her mother's place. My mother did not want me to be between the problems that will be there with her sister and brothers. So, I stay with my father even when he marries another wife. My father passes away last year, many of his things he had and the policies things go to my stepmother. I was gived R10 000 qha! So, one day my stepmother comes to my room at the back of the home, she say she is selling the house, and I must go somewhere, I must find a place of me to stay. So I see that there is nothing for me here, no employment I can get, I buyed bus ticket to here and think I will get opportunity for some work. I have been here for some months, and all the money I was gived is finishing and I need a work at least, even if it pays not many money. It's tough, kweli rhawuti; we just must keep going.'

This story Mavusi related to me on a particular somber morning when I was reading a newspaper article about a woman who killed her husband so she could claim life policies. Apparently, this was the third husband that passed away while married to this woman.

A lot of things change when a person's parent passes away, a lot of things happen in families when people divorce, and in many cases, children are the greatly affected parties. Children, if they are still young, are constantly faced with decisions of where they will be spending the weekend or the school holidays. In other cases, the poor children are used by parents and families as tools to fight each other. They become casualties of a love gone totally wrong.

Sthibo on the other hand has a typical story of a township kid who made bad decisions that resulted in him dropping out of school. Drugs, alcohol, and women are what led him to this corner. He epitomizes the story of the protagonist that is sung about in Teargas's old-time classic song *Chance*, where the tragic character laments the past decisions that have brought him gloom.

Today I am seating in the front passenger seat with my two other cadres at the back of the bakkie. I am in most cases seated in the front passenger seat, especially if our employer for the day is a white person like today. It is like this because I am more fluent in English than many who inhabit our corner looking for employment. I was not initially aware that the reason most times my cadres avoided the front passenger seat was because of the language barrier. Many of these gentlemen were not privileged enough to reach institutions of higher learning, in fact, most of them did not even finish school.

I am the anomaly of the cult: I completed my matric and went to college where I studied electrical engineering and obtained my N6 certificate.

I had believed that upon completion of my studies I would get employment and have a better life, education is the key to success, that is the anthem. But life is unpredictable.

When I left my village in the Northern Cape coming here, I had big dreams for the future, but they have not manifested how I had hoped. My dreams continue to corrode and vanish. Upon the completion of my studies here, I knew that going back home was not an option. There was nothing for me there, no opportunities whatsoever, and so I made a tough decision of continuing my stay here in this foreign province. Here, I believed that I could attain employment, but three years later I still have not. I have no idea how many curriculum vitae I have submitted without ever even getting an interview.

The car cuts across N4, I have lost count of the number of traffic lights we have crossed. I have since been looking out the window afraid to glance in the direction of my employer for the day. I always make it a point to never start conversations with my employers, I believe it to be a sign of respect. He has been on his phone talking to someone.

'Nee(No), dis heeltemal onaanvaarbaar (that is totally unacceptable). As die goed nie more daar is nie, gaan dit n probleem wees (I need those things delivered tomorrow or we are going to have a problem). Die mense is veronderstel om binne sewe dae in te trek (These people are supposed to move into this

house in seven days). As julle nie die diens kan lewer nie, dan moet jy nou vir my se sodat ek n betroubare voorskaffer kan kry (If you cannot deliver tell me now so I can call a reliable supplier)', he had said to whoever was on the other side before he paused to listen to the reply.

'Okay, now you're talking, see you soon bye', he said to the person on the other end before he hung up his phone and grabbed a box of cigarettes and lit one.

'Do you mind if I smoke?' he asked after taking a puff. I suspected he did not care if I minded or not, he was merely asking for the sake of it. He would have asked before even igniting one if he really wanted my opinion.

'No sir I don't mind', I timidly said trying very hard to force a smile.

'So, what's your name?' he asks smoke oozing out of his mouth and nostrils.

'Me? I am Thapelo' timidly I say.

'What does that mean?'

'Praying... sorry, prayer I mean, it means prayer'. There seems to be this fear that is overcoming me as I speak to this gentleman.

Tokelo Hlagala.

'I will call you Prayer, Tapelu is a difficult name, he utters with stern authority.
...' Your friends, what are their names?'.
I recognize he is not even willing to make an effort to learn my name, but this is nothing new here. I have encountered such in a variety of ways. The most shocking was when I came across some fellow black people who could not pronounce my name correctly.

I want to tell him that Mavusi, Sthibo, and I are not really friends, that we met at the corner, and we hustle together, and I don't even know their surnames. But I suspect he does not want to know the nature of our friendship, nor does he care what we mean to each other, or whether I know their surnames.

'Mavusi and Sthibo. Sthibo is the one with the cap, and Mavusi is the one with chiskop'. He glances at the back through his mirror to connect the names to the characterization I have articulated. He does not entertain me with a reply, merely continues smoking his cigarette. The smoke is affecting me, and I feel like coughing, but I can't, he might regard it as disrespect. He increases the volume of his radio, he is listening to Jacaranda Fm.

Poor Folk/s.

As I glance at the back Mavusi and Sthibo seem to be having a nice chat, I suspect they are talking about women. Sthibo is probably telling Mavusi about a new woman he met over the weekend. Sthibo is the Casanova of all the gentlemen that I am familiar with at the corner.

We are now entering a mall and the car comes to a stop. *'I will be back, stay here'*, before I can respond with an *'okay'*, he has already shut the door and walking towards the mall. Mavusi and Sthibo knock on the window and ask me what is going on. I tilt my head showing them I don't know.

I am wondering to myself what sort of job we are going to do today. Will it be painting: will it be gardening? Will it be cleaning the yard? Will it be cleaning windows? Will it be moving things? Will it be washing trucks? The last idea is rare.

'These damn cashiers don't know how to do their job', these are the utterances our employer said immediately when he sat down in the driver seat. Something must have transpired inside the shop that annoyed him.

Tokelo Hlagala.

As usual, I did not reply, I was not certain as to what facial expression to deploy regarding his remarks. He had six cans of Redbull and a packet of cigarettes.

We finally arrive at a newly built house where there are still a few men working, they seem to be installing electric cables. We alight the car.

'Vhusana, which one is Vhusana again?', I point to Mavusi.

'Yes, you will be working with Prayer, that pile of grass must be laid on the ground, those trees must be planted in places where I will show you just now'. We nodded to everything he was saying.

'You, the other one, I forgot your name, you will be working with me on the other side, come let's go I will show you then come back to show them'.

Sthibo and the white man who did not tell us his name, and no one of us would dare ask disappeared to the back of the house.

Wisdom cannot be attained by one without earning their lot– of winters and shivers in this world. The wise are patient and endure hardships. But how long must one stay patient? How long will the storm dance around me? Does it not know it affects those that are near and dear to my heart even though they are miles away? Does it not fathom the ripple effects of its existence on generations to come?

Wealth is generational, so is poverty, with this limited time if my fate does not change the generation post me will suffer the same ills. They will have to climb the same hills, combat the same existential bondage.

I wonder during many sleepless nights, where is the bearer of my treasures?

Today is Wednesday, on Monday and Tuesday we went to work with that white man whose name remains a mystery to us, and chances are it will forever be. He had hoped that we could manage to complete the job he had for us in a single day, but he had underestimated the amount of work it was, so we went on Tuesday and completed the work.

By 12:00 we had completed, after paying us in brown envelopes he drove us back to this corner of ours where he found us, returning tools utilized to the exact spot they were found.

Tokelo Hlagala.

We knew there was no way someone would come looking for workers after 12:00 and so we decided to go to our places of residence, but before that, we passed at liquor city to grab a few beers to thank ourselves for a job well done.

For many of us in the township, alcohol has become a central part of our lives, it Is what we use to drown our sorrows, drinking away the pain of not being in alignment with our dreams. As much as we were celebrating the work we did, we were lowkey drinking away the pain of this line of work, the constant struggle for survival.

My fate today, in this chilly morning, is unknown. It is 06:00 and no car has come yet.

It is now 07:30 and no car has stopped by looking for workers.

It is now 08:00 still no sign of light.
It is now 11:00 and the other gentlemen have begun going back home, they have lost hope of getting any employment for the day.

Poor Folk/s.

It is now 12:00, I know for a fact that no one is going to come henceforth, but I do not go back to my place of residence. I do not want to go. Going to my room means I will arrive and eat lunch; I do not have enough food. So, I decide to stay with Mavusi here, we are the only ones left. I am not certain why Mavusi is not going home, but I know for me it is my grocery status. Maybe he too fears something where he stays, is it maybe an empty fridge like me? Is he perhaps avoiding his landlord regarding the rent that he was supposed to pay? Or is he merely afraid of the thoughts that come to his mind when he is isolated and alone? It could be one of these reasons, or something different.

Cars come to a temporary pause at the traffic lights near us, and they pass. Some are lucky when they approach the lights are green. They thank God for their luck and pass swiftly to their different destinations.

Some of the drivers and passengers that pass by look at us with pity, some with disdain, some look, and smile, as if they are trying to brighten our days and compensate for our struggles. Some look at us with a smile of pity. Some don't even recognize our existence.

Tokelo Hlagala.

I have witnessed many things in this corner of the world, I have seen car collisions. I have witnessed road rage among drivers, we had to intervene many times to calm the situation.

I have seen accidents where we were the primary respondents even before the emergency services, many times we were the ones that called them. I have seen blood spill: people lose their lives because of one person's carelessness and disregard for the rules of the road. I have seen quite a lot, but the memories and traumas of this corner quickly vanish, and we focus on our quest, we continue our uphill climb like Sisyphus, and we carry our burdens.

Every day I wish I could be like many of these people that pass with their cars in the morning going to work, that I could wear some of these beautiful uniforms that they are wearing. With the progression of time, the little hope of reaching my goals ebbs away from me. It seems that my academic toil was in vain, I was told that education is the key, but it hasn't opened any doors for me.

My mother took the last few cents that she received when my father passed away and sent me to school so I would be able to help my three siblings. But it seems those last few cents were spent in vain. Whenever I think back to my mother's words which she said to me when I left home to start college, I break into tears.

'My child, you see that your father is no more. The little money that we received when he passed away, I have used to build us this three-room house, so that your siblings and I can have some privacy. I have also used some of the money to get us the things that we need, and I have then paid the society in advance at least for a year, so should there be anything happening to me they will be able to bury me. You can see I am in ill health; you my son will have to be the Moses of this family. With this little remaining money, I am sending you to school. If you get there and play with this money and do things that risk your academics, know that you are playing with the future of this family, the future of your siblings'.

These words have stuck with me for a very long time. I never engaged in any behaviors that would jeopardize my academics in college because of these words. I spent endless nights burning the midnight oil in order to get good grades, but all this seems to have been in vain. I have nothing to show for all that hard work.

I have not called my mother in weeks, not because I do not afford airtime, but because I cannot bring myself to talk to her. I feel that I have failed her, she had placed all her trust in me that I would save the family from poverty, that through my efforts my siblings would have a bright future. I had believed when I left home that I was going to be the Moses of the family, but I am not. There used to be times where I could call her and tell her the problems that I was facing, this was when I was still a student, but since I graduated, I do not tell her anything, I feel she has enough problems already.

There is really no one that I can share my frustrations with. I used to be a churchgoer. When I came here, I brought with me my church uniform and used to go to church, but months or so after graduation I stopped going to church. In all honesty, I am furious at God. I feel like raising my fist at him and cursing him for forsaking me. I have always lived a virtuous life, but here I am, nowhere in life.

Poor Folk/s.

I have lost friends due to unemployment: I have distanced myself from others because I cannot afford the places, they want us to go to. I have lost relationships because of my fiscal status. I have been single for over a year. Why would I want to bring another person into my poverty? A man is known as a provider, I cannot provide for myself, I cannot provide for my family, why add someone else into this mess.

The earliest bird catches the firstest worm, an adage used to promote time and timing. This adage has been proven wrong many times in my line of work. There are days where you're first at the intersection and others come after you, but luck just happens to be on their side. A bakkie stopping just as they cross the road to join you, with you still seated down surveying the expanse, they are at an advantage, they are nearer, they are already in motion.

Today was a bad day. As I place my work suites in my wardrobe after a bad day, I see my formal wear suite hanging purposelessly as if it is being lynched by an owner who does not appreciate its existence. This suit has been

Tokelo Hlagala.

worn once, it is the suit that allowed me to make a grand entrance during graduation, it is the suit that I believed I would only wear for job interviews. Sadly, interviews have hidden from me like the earth hides from the sun in the nighttime.

Months and months have passed, the dust has even settled on its shoulders corroding its fabric. To me, this suit is a reminder of a cracked and crippled dream, a dream that continues to crack creating a gorge between itself and its owner. Where my qualification once hung, now it's an empty wall, with a nail protruding as a sign that there was once something hung on this wall, a dream hung, but a dream deferred– possibly deceased.
A nauseating feeling brewed within me every time I woke up for my unskilled labor pursuit and I saw it hanging by the wall. I felt betrayed, it was the one key that was supposed to open doors for me, but the doors remain shut and firmly protected.

Like sands through the hourglass so are the days of our lives, the days seem to pass by painfully slow, but the months– the months painfully fast. There is still mist and frost shrouding my future, the possibilities of the morrow are bleak, and with each passing day modicum of hope drips. The axiom 'all shall be well' has been overused and has worn out.

In this line of work winters are loathed by many, but the hustle must continue come rain, come sunshine.

Today is another day, Monday the 20th of June, the sun has not shown its nose and it appears it might be a cloudy morning. It is right in the belly of winter and cold air is molesting my face, hardening my nose and ears, mucus continues its adventure and attempts to free itself from nostril bondage. I forgot my gloves and beanie at one of the places we had found work at, at the beginning of June.

I cannot go and collect them, for I don't even know the name of that place, it is some affluent suburbs I had never been to before. Even if I knew the place– when I arrive at the security, who will I say I am looking for? Who is that lady's name? like usual I had not asked her, we had not spoken throughout the journey. At this current moment, I do not afford to buy new ones, I will have to endure the blistering winter.

Today the closest of my comrades, Mavusi and Sthibo, are not here. Mavusi came on Thursday, he was not feeling well. On Friday he came again, and his condition had worsened, I suspect he got worse. Sthibo on the other hand gives himself breaks on very cold mornings. I understand that unlike me and Mavusi, he has a home, he stays with his mother and father, and so whether he comes to work or not, he will still have a roof over his head. Sthibo's privileges are not extended to me and Mavusi, he and I are always one paycheck away from being homeless, we do not have the luxury of pulling the blanket over our heads on Mondays we feel are too cold, on days we feel like our bodies have been beaten and battered enough by the previous toil.

Today we are in luck and there's only me and two other gentlemen who I have seen here but never spoke to.

At 07:00 a bakkie comes to a stop, we all stand up but are a bit hesitant to run towards the car. We know the type of bakkies that are looking for us, and this one is too lavish. The driver slides down his double cab window car and calls us. As we approach the bakkie the driver says,

'Get in guys, it is cold out here'. This he said with an affable tone. The gentleman humbly escorts and gestures us in.

Likewise, I take the front passenger seat.

'Can you guys' paint?'

'Yes, we can'. I speak on behalf of everyone. My two other comrades gesture a yes with their heads.

'Cool, let's go'. Says the kind-looking gentleman who is soon to be our new temporal boss for that day.

He sets the car in motion towards our workplace for the day. I am sure I have had a lot of workplaces in comparison to the average person. Today I know the type of work from the word go. I am happy with the job. In my experience, we usually take three to four days to paint a house. The people that come here usually live in double and triple-story houses, so I know I have employment for a minimum of three days.

Tokelo Hlagala.

'Let me turn on the heater for you guys, you must be freezing hey', he speaks again in a polite manner.

'Yes sir, it is very freezing out there', again I reply on behalf of my comrades, likewise they nod and smile to show they agree.

'No, no, please don't call me sir, I am Tom, just Tom', he utters with a smile concluding his remarks.

'Just Tom it is. And I am Thapelo' I reply.

Today for some reason unknown, I have no reservations about having a conversation with my employer.

'And who are your friends?' he inquires glancing at them for a second.

I do not know the names of these comrades of mine, but before I can say anything I am saved from the humiliation of not knowing their names.

'I am Benedict' one of my comrades says.

'And I am Velaphi' the other follows.

'Good to meet you gentlemen, and what does Velaphi mean?' he further inquiries, it seems it is the first time he comes across this name. It is only now that I realize even though this employer of ours for the day is white, he is

Poor Folk/s.

not a South African, his accent sounds British. *'Mystery solved'* I say to myself.

'Velaphi means, where do you come from' I reply on behalf of my comrade suspecting that from his look, he doesn't fully understand what this man is asking, or he did not hear him well.

'Mhh interesting' he replies.

The car cuts through several suburbs and we come to a stop at his house.
We are shown what the task of the day will be, we are shown the paints, one orange, the other grey, and there are brushes and a ladder on the side. Before we start with the job for the day we are led into another room.

'Here is breakfast gentleman, tea, coffee, muffins, biscuits, whatever you want, help yourself out, I will be back shortly.'

We spend a good three days working with this affable gentleman. He would bring us lunch, and engage us during the lunch period, asking us where we come from, and all these questions that we tend to ask new people we meet. I was very sad on our last day when he dropped us back to our famous, notorious to some, corner.

I knew that chances were that I would never see him again, I would never be spoiled to breakfast before I start working, and brought food during lunch, and asked if I needed the heater. I was sad to see him go, but I knew his kindness would forever be ingrained in my heart, it is very rare in this line of our work to meet such people.

Many of the people who pick us up for work look down on us, you can see from how they look at us, how they scan us, how they can't wait to clean their car seats when we alight.

I recall there was one gentleman who made us seat at the back of the bakkie on a cold morning even though there was space in the other seats, it was extremely cold, and cloudy, and it began to drizzle.

This gentleman, Tom, is a rare breed amongst the aristocrats that we serve. He took my phone number for future work opportunities, but I suspect he was only trying to give us hope.

Poor Folk/s.

It has been over 10 days since we worked with Tom. Since then, I have not received any employment. One Wednesday a bakkie came and the gentlemen ran towards it, to seize the opportunity. I was peeing by the tree. Upon turning to make my way towards my comrades, I saw the buttocks of the bakkie, the car releasing gas and delivering my comrades to their paycheck. I was heavily saddened by this, I had just turned my back for three mere seconds, that was all it took for me to miss an opportunity for employment. Nothing further came that day and I went home with a sore heart.

The next day a bakkie came and I ran as fast as I could, I was the first one to arrive at the bakkie. *'I need painters'*, the lady had said. *'Yes, I can paint'*, I need only two. Before I could ascend into the car, I realized I had forgotten my bag where I was seated, I quickly made a run for the bag, upon turning back the car was no more. Another bad day, another sad day it was.

I sat down and the fourth guy that was part of us when we ran to the car also walked back disappointed. He sat beside me, and we began to have a conversation, he was perhaps three months into this hustle. His name was Victor, but he was not a victor today, like me.

Victor told me he comes from Malawi, and before he arrived in South Africa he had travelled to Zambia and stayed there for a while, then travelled to Zimbabwe where he stayed for almost a year hustling odd jobs here and there. When he made enough money, he crossed over to South Africa and has been looking for some odd jobs here and there. Victor had complained about the economic state of his country, but the tipping point that made him cut through two countries coming to South Africa was the political tension in his country where there were rebels fighting for territory with the government. He had lost his family when the rebels invaded his village. There was nothing for him to stay there for. His was just like the story of many people who came from different countries hoping to make something of their lives.

Eventually, we parted ways, I had learned another story about another comrade. We were facing the same life predicament; we

Poor Folk/s.

both had been hurt by the happenings of the morning that did not favor us. We did not get any employment for the next couple of days, but our stories intersected.

Destinies are hung over our heads by our milieu, we walk with them overhead, they are our shadows that never leave our side. Some choose to overlook and pretend that they do not have them, but mine I cannot. Every minute of each day as I stand at this corner, cornered by poverty, I am reminded that mine is to overcome poverty and the ills that it brings.

Every day I am reminded that the progress of my family and lineage is hanging over my shoulders. Do I have the dexterity to overcome this adversity? I was a promising child, from ever since I can recall, my mother told me I was destined for greatness, my teachers gave me the look, *'you will achieve great things'*. I remember the many times my father took me to his workplace.

How he would brag about how smart I was, *'this is your smart child?'* his colleagues would ask whenever I visited.

Tokelo Hlagala.

The burden of a destiny, how I long to make him proud in his grave, how I wish he could have left his grave vacant for a few more years, perhaps I would not be carrying this proverbial weight.

It's Friday, winter is ebbing, both Mavusi and Sthibo are here with me. Mavusi recovered some days ago. A car comes to a stop not far from us. We run to the car, I miss my step and fall on the pavement, but I dust myself up quickly and climb the bakkie to our work for the day, there is no time to nurse bruises, the wheel must turn, and I must be inside that car as it does.

Today is Monday, it is 10:00. Very rarely am I in my room at this time of the day on a Monday. It is not by choice that I am here but through unfortunate circumstances. I woke up at 05:00 with the purpose of preparing for my hustle. Upon waking I realize that my ankle is very swollen, it has been very painful since the fall I took on Friday, but today the condition is appalling, I cannot even wear a shoe. I have

Poor Folk/s.

no choice but to put some ice and hope the swelling will be gone tomorrow.

It is Wednesday today, the swelling of my ankle persists, the pain seems to worsen, I haven't been going to work. I am beginning to worry, if this leg persists, I will not have a place to stay next month. I will not afford to pay for accommodation; I may not even afford to have food.

It is Friday today. I went to the clinic, the pain had become unbearable, and the swelling had not subsided. The nurse gave me some medication and told me that I should not go to work for the next three weeks.

'*Are you employed?*' the nurse had asked post examining my ankle.

'*Yes, I work in construction*' I said.

'*Nice*' she replied with a smile.

I was glad that she did not ask which company I worked for, or what it was that I did exactly in the company that I worked at. I could have not told her the type of work that I did, that it was employment by chance, by the grace of God, that it depended on how fast I could run to seize the opportunity. I could not have told her that I do not have a pay slip, that I could not apply for leave, that even this injury on duty was not paid for.

I could not have told her that in most of the jobs that I did, I did not know the type of work I would be doing till I arrived at the location. I really could not have told her that I did not know the location of my workstation till the car arrived at the destination. I really could not have told her that, chances are that over 90 percent of my past employers only see me once or twice, and I am erased from their memories once the paint in their houses dries and brightens, once the lawns and trees in their garden grow. I could not tell her the nature of my employment had she wanted to know exactly what it entailed. I was glad her curiosity was limited.

'Unfortunately, Abuti, you will not be able to go to work for the next three weeks, your ankle is very damaged, good thing you came in when you did, few more days you would have done great damage.'

When she said those words the only thoughts that flooded my mind were, 'what will I eat?

Poor Folk/s.

where will I stay? I do not have money, it has been a very bad month, I had hoped my luck would change in the next couple of days'.

It is Saturday the 30th, I have been sparring the food I have, it will only last me for a week max. From my bed I see our landlady's car coming in, she is coming to collect the rent, what will I say to her? what will I give her? I have no money.

'Knock knock'

I open the door...

Tokelo Hlagala.

Poor Folk/s.

...The world has become an Island and I find island comfortable residing in my broken heart for I too deviate from humanity.
I am the poor folk!

For whom the bell tolls.

'Yes, table for one'.

We are born into the world without our consent, or perhaps that is not absolutely true. The fact that we won the spermatozoa race just might be an antithesis to the idea that we are born without our consent. But one thing that is almost certain is that we do not choose our milieu. The types of environments and social backgrounds we are born into, the familial structures that we find already erected, the legacies of wealth or deprivation in our lineage. For some their milieus are a great blessing, and for some not, *I am uncertain of mine*, the chaos I spend years trying to put into order.

Tokelo Hlagala.

Sounds indicate actions and potential events; they call to attention those who are listening. A beep of a phone call's attention to the receiver, an ambulance siren calls the attention of the motorists on the road, thunder indicates rain. With all sounds, we can determine what is transpiring, or imminent.

There was a sound in my youth that send pangs into my stomach, it is a sound I had no choice but to endure for half a decade, a sound of a tolling bell.

This bell tolled five days a week, always at the exact times. It tolled 10 times daily, akin the rising sun it was never late. I am not certain where it was positioned, but regardless of where I was seated during the period of its toll, I would hear it as if it was humming at the back of my ear.

There was a point in time when I was still schooling somewhere in the north part of the country. In that school there was a designated individual who would go around signaling what time it was with the manual bell– that it was time for the start of the schooling, that it was time to change periods, that it was time to go to lunch, and that finally, it was time to occlude matters for the day.

Poor Folk/s.

The bell that was used in that part of the country was similar to the manual bells that are usually attached to livestock– with the purpose of making it easier for a shepherd to locate his livestock when in the wilderness. They would simply follow the sound and pinpoint the location of their livestock, this was a herding innovation, but at the same time, the sounds indicated to wild animals the direction of the livestock. As much as it made it easier for the shepherd to locate his livestock, it simultaneously offered the privilege of potential death from wild animals.

The make-up of the environment where this school was situated, was a small village which at that time did not have electricity, running water, and tar roads. It is at this school that I was introduced to systemic learning. Electricity did arrive a year or so after my relocation, tar roads did arrive much later, perhaps over 10 years later. But as for running water, even today it remains nonexistent. The villagers used to collect water from the nearest river, *Hlakaro* river. I have gone to collect water at this particular river a few times in my childhood. On

Tokelo Hlagala.

my side, it was not as a result of necessity, but a mere excuse for some adventure. *Hlakaro* river, therefore, was the first idea of what an ocean felt like. I was young at the time, so the only time I was allowed to go to the river was with aid and guidance from the elderly siblings or neighbors. Unfortunately, with growing pollution, the practice of water collection from rivers and wells has since died out because of health precautions. As a result, many resorted to boreholes, with those who do not afford to have boreholes depending on the communal water that is delivered through the shared taps within the community.

It is these sounds of bells that remind me of the different epochs and moments in my life. Once there was an old man in my neighborhood, he sold ice cream. He would toll his bell around the neighborhood exactly during the times when we would be playing in the streets. His bell was the manual one similar to the one that was used at my first school.
Quickly everything would come to a temporal halt when this old man came tolling his bell descending third avenue. Third Avenue was the street that separated Mandela extension 1

informal settlement with extension 2 where it was bond houses. This is where children from both classes met for play.

Whatever we would be playing would come to a stop, be it soccer, or *hide & seek*– with *hide & seek* never-ending well, it always ended because someone was unhappy with how others were playing. An argument would ensue, verbal never physical, and before we knew it the game was over. We knew very well never to have any physical altercations, things would get extremely nasty for all of us if that transpired, we would all be punished. The unsettling part about growing up in the township was that it did not even have to be our parents who punished us for the misdemeanor. Any elderly person passing by had a community–parenting right to discipline any misdemeanors, whether they knew the child or not, that is perhaps why we never misbehaved radically. This simple social practice kept us in check.

So, our leisurely play and recreation would come to a halt as the ice cream man descended our street. Our playmates would run to the ice cream man to purchase some ice cream, it was as though they had come prepared for his arrival. Some would quickly run to their homes where they would be collecting the money they had saved. Some would run to ask from their elders. The monetary requests of some were met with grace and they received, but some came back with pale faces, their shoulders slacking, and their eyes teary because their requests were declined. They would be engulfed by disappointment and disdain. Others on the other hand didn't even come back to play until later or the next day. They did not want to make that long walk of shame back. The greatly unfortunate ones would be given a chore upon arriving home before they could even begin the mission of what they had run home to do. A few others and I would continue playing, pretending as if we didn't hear the bell, nor see the old man. We knew we came from families where ice cream was luxury, it was frivolous niceties for those that came from families that had a better financial background.

I often wondered what happened to the old man who brought gloom to the likes of me. At some point in time, he stopped passing by. I am not sure if he found another niche, another highly profitable neighborhood, or maybe his

Poor Folk/s.

business went bankrupt, and even business rescue initiatives were rendered obsolete to aid his business, or maybe he got a job somewhere. Although I doubt that he may have got a job, he seemed very old, it would not be ideal to hire him in my estimation, he would soon be gone, and I know corporations do a vast risk assessment before hiring anyone. But I suspect also that he was not as old as he appeared– as we thought. There is something coldly uniform I have realized, poverty and depravation makes many appear way older than they are, whereas money can prolong one's youth.

The conclusion that I reached was that he may have been a victim of the harsh goddess of death, that he may have passed away. I am aware that the statement I am about to make may appear inhumane, but I was very glad that he was no longer there. I was glad that his bell would no longer torment the likes of myself, that we would no longer have to salivate as other kids artistically licked their ice creams from the bottom rising to the pinnacle of the cream. I was glad that my tastebuds would no longer have to cringe from envy.

Tokelo Hlagala.

At 07:40 the bell rang, signaling the start of the school day, that all learners had to assemble at the school assembly. At 14:00 a bell rang, it signaled the end of the schooling day, that learners and teachers were now free to leave the school yard. But in between these two bell tolls there was two significant tolls, one of which brought me utmost gloom, the other which brought me some modicum of relief. The first was the tolling bell which signified lunch period, for me it meant break period. This significant bell tolled at exactly 11;00, at this point four periods had lapsed for the day, it tolled a bit louder and longer than the three others prior, but not more than the first one in the morning. Lunch time...break time, this period for me meant a moment to get out of the classroom and get some fresh air, stretch my legs a bit before enduring the remaining four periods of the day.

Lunchtime postulates that one is about to feast on that which they are carrying for the day, or they are going to visit the school tuck-shop and in the buffet of meals, drinks and snacks decide what their stomach craves. But for me... for me it was one of the periods that reminded me of where I came from. It was one of the periods where reality hit me in the face like frosty air molesting the face of a Mount Everest climber. This period reminded me that I came from a household of deprivation and economic degradation, that the fiscal standing in the household that I was from did not allow me to carry not even R2 that could afford me a snack, or an apple to keep the doctor in the making awake.

One might have interrogated and asked, *'why do you not carry a lunch pack?'* 'How could I? When I hardly had enough for supper, when rooibos tea is what filled the other compartments of my stomach that had not received food for the night. How could I? When there were days where even that mere rooibos was nonexistent, and water would take the duty with piety'.

I dreaded this period of the day greatly. I internally lamented its arrival and celebrated its departure akin how one who resides in a leaking house loathes the arrival of rain and jubilates as it fades, and the rainbow illuminates the sky. I often thought of crafting a petition that I would take to all learners mobilizing them in convincing the school to cancel the lunch period, for it was not me

Tokelo Hlagala.

alone who suffered during this period, but I knew that would remain a dream.

There were others, many like me who I knew dreaded this period of the day, but they would not openly voice it out, for I too never voiced it out openly. That's the thing with poverty, it robs one of their voice, it robs one of their dignity, the same way rape takes away the voice and dignity of the victim, many like me were silent victims.

It is difficult to share our sufferings with the world of people who do not know firsthand how the experience feels like. It is almost equally difficult to even engage people who share our sufferings, we feel vulnerable and naked.

Often, I used to pretend as though I had a lot of work, and I would be glued to my books during this period so that people would not see nor inquire as to why I was not eating lunch as others. I sadly could not openly block my nose from the stench of the bunny chows, the aroma of the chips that would hit me in the face, the aroma ascending into the depth of my nostrils, my thoughts salivating as others feasted around me. *'If only I could afford'* I wept internally.

Poor Folk/s.

I've got friends, my clique at school which encompasses mainly of those that come from well off standing families. Every time during this lunch period I disappeared from my friends, so they could locate me not. They have never noticed my patterns of disappearances, and that's the thing with privilege, it doesn't offer the privileged a lens of seeing what those without are seeing and experiencing, *by virtue of having he thinks*, 'others have too'.

There was this friend of mine, Moshe, who came from an even greater pit of poverty than I, perhaps that is why I and him grew so close over time. I understood where he came from, and he too understood where I came from. Although we didn't openly speak about the places we came from, somehow, we spoke through some grand forces, birds of a feather flocking together, and he was my kind of bird.

Necessity is said to be a fuel for invention. As a result, I cultivated a strategy that would keep me consumed during the lunch period, a strategy to keep me going through rough terrains, through unforgiving troughs.

Luckily this time I had the resources to make this idea manifest. Having a soccer ball that a friend had left at my house at one point in time, I decided to carry with me this soccer ball daily to school, there and then during the lunch breaks, me and my depraved cult would be in the field of play sweating our lungs out playing soccer. It wasn't really in the field of play, but the assembly spot where we would be playing as if we were at Old Trafford with the world watching.

Only we were not at old Trafford, we were at the school assembly, only it was not a thousand spectators, but a few 100 other learners watching while simultaneously keeping their jaws occupied, grinding and chewing what they had brought and bought from the school tuck shop. This practice became my escape from the face of poverty, it became a methodology that I could use to overcome the struggle that I was faced with.

When the follow-up bell tolled, I took a deep breath, for my ordeal and many others like me had ended. I'm not really sure what happened to those who had not crafted a perfect plan like mine. But even so, when we returned for the remaining half of the day there was still the stench of what was being feasted on, but the aroma did not equate to seeing others keeping their mouths occupied while all

Poor Folk/s.

you could do is talk, with the purpose of preventing one's mouth from growing a bad breath while those of others had a scent of whatever they feasted on.

There was another kind of day that I dreaded, that equated to my daily lunch torments. I am certain that there were many others who dreaded this day deeper than me. It is when we were instructed to wear casual clothes. It was usually on a Friday when there was some sort of holiday or theme that was being celebrated. It could have been Valentine's Day: it could have been Heritage Day or any among the multitude of holidays that exist in the South African calendar. These were such days when other learners went into their walk-in closets and pulled out their finest pair of shoes, their finest garments which they would, during the course of the day, brag about, narrating the tales of the genesis of their brands, narrating how Nike was made in Vietnam, how Chuck Taylor created one of the finest sneakers– Converse All-star. These would be the type of conversations that echoed in different classrooms throughout the day, the juxtaposition of garments and brands. I dreaded this day– for my clothes only occupied one shelf in our broken wardrobe. As

Tokelo Hlagala.

for shoes, my parents had purchased me two
pairs of Grasshoppers shoes, one black for
school purposes and church, the other,
brownish looking like for purposes outside
school and church– social events. My mother
had bought them at *Marabastad,* she brought
them because they could last one a lifetime,
thus avoiding the constant back-to-back
purchase of shoes, especially school shoes
since I played roughly at school. I vowed then
that none of my kids would ever own these
hideous pair of shoes. Of course, they were not
really hideous, but picture you are deserted in
a jungle somewhere, where the only food
available is Guavas. Furthermore, picture that
you are deserted for months, and in that
period the only thing you can depend on for
nutrition are the Guavas, what kind of
relationship would you develop with them?
Although they may have been what sustained
you in need, you will not want to ever eat them
again. That is my relationship with grasshopper
shoes. To make matters worse, we had to pay
R2 for wearing the casual clothes, even if you
were wearing the school uniform. It was part of
some fundraising initiative for the school, raising
funds for the school while I had nothing in my
pocket, what an irony.

Poor Folk/s.

At one point in time when we were requested to do an unprepared speech, I almost wanted to echo this subject matter, but I stuttered when I had to speak, I tried to open my mouth, but nothing came out. The subject matter was still too close to my heart, fragile, it was still a wound that I did not want to reveal to the world.

Sometimes when we are going through certain trials and tribulations, it is extremely hard to write, not to mention speak about them. I realized at that moment that it would make me naked to the entire world, the entire classroom. I realized that I would be the talk of the town, well! The talk of the classroom, or worse– people would start feeling pity for me, and even though I understood the circumstances of where I came from. I did not want a pity party, charity from the world or Messiahs' manna.

Pride was the only thing I could afford in that circumstance, now I can afford a whole lot.

Sipping this chardonnay and devouring this celestial omelet from this beautiful rooftop view of the richest square mile in Africa, I reminisce on past memories. I reminisce on what was once my life– I wonder, had I been born in a

Tokelo Hlagala.

different background than the one I was–
would I have been driven as I have been? to
achieve the wealth that I today have
attained? Was lack and depravation the fuel
that I needed to push me to these great
heights?

Has my fate of becoming a great footballer
today been a direct impact of all those
countless lunch periods playing my poverty
away while others enjoyed delicacies?

*'One must have chaos in oneself to
give birth to a dancing star.'*

Poor Folk/s.

Better and different childhood and adulthood.
A different environment.
Better and improved mental health.
Physical strength to carry on when the mountain
becomes steeper.
A fair and just society...

How will it happen?

The genesis of certain demeanors and changes in demeanors can at times be never fully understood. This is, especially if they are of others and not ourselves. We are eternal mysteries to ourselves. We progressively in modicums reveal ourselves to ourselves. This is through our thoughts and many times through our actions, but there are certain things that remain locked up in the deeper recesses of our being. Like onions, time and circumstances peel our layers at a time.

My husband became a mystery as time unfolded and certain layers of him were uncovered.

Tokelo Hlagala.

Everything in our household was flowing flawlessly and fluently. Of course, every household and marriage have their own hiccups and challenges here and there, now and then, but overall, we were not plagued by any proverbial unending maladies. But things changed, his behavior changed.

It is not yet dark, but the darkness is fast approaching as night looms, the twilight has already sunk in the west and shadows are now to the east.

It has been a long day, I am yawning, and it is increasingly growing difficult to keep my eyes open, I am very exhausted.

I woke before the sunrise, early before the chickens could announce the imminence of the morning, by the time they echoed their screams I was already halfway sweeping the yard, and the dust was bellowing. I knew there was a great deal to be done, the earlier the better. Few of my neighbors echoed their greetings as they passed by heading to their diverse workplaces. Like a good neighbor I greeted them back to maintain a good communal reputation adhering to the standards and creeds of humanity, 'love and *care for thy neighbor'* or at least pretend to, I paid my neighborly dues and greeted back.

A few children who I presume to be in matric also greeted me humbly like children are taught to. Like a caring mother even though I did not know some of them, I respectfully greeted them back.

Memories of my own youth flashed, memories of when I was still in school and greatly hopeful about my future, my aspirations to become a teacher or nurse.

I grew up in a household where my father was the breadwinner and I never for a day saw my mother go to work, she was a housewife, a submissive housewife who I felt many a times was disregarded by my father. He cared about neither her opinion nor feelings. It was during that phase that I felt I did not want to be in a similar marriage, voiceless, I wanted to have a voice, a career in teaching. I felt it could give me that in many ways, that I would not be disregarded because I depended on a man to provide.

Post sweeping, I began to wash all the curtains and blankets in the house, by this time I had woken the children to join the movement and work for their daily meal.

Tokelo Hlagala.

As a vanguard against dirt, we turned everything upside down cleaning. My kids, oh my poor kids, they have spent all day helping me with these chores, when I was washing the curtains, they were washing the windows. When I was sweeping the yard, they were moving the pile of bricks that were left next to the entrance by the builders, they did not look neat there and so I told the kids to move them to the back.

Several wheelbarrow journeys later they had completed the removal task, and it looks so clean and clear now. I was afraid that rats might start creating their homes here and end up intruding into the house. I hate rats, and these small reptiles, they usually house themselves where there is a pile of bricks or debris.

By luck, we finished everything we had set our eyes on. Tomorrow is Sunday, maybe I might tell them to bunk church as I feel they are very tired. I am sure they will be very elated to bunk church, these kids of mine do not like church on Sundays. They have no problem with going during the week, the only problem is Sunday. On many days I make them go under duress, but tomorrow I might just be a bad mother and let them bunk, surely, they will not be rejected from the kingdom of God for missing church this one time.

Night has finally established itself and won the tug of war against day. The constellations of stars are getting brighter and brighter as the depth of the night drives deeper, and the earth hides itself further and further from the sun, the dust has settled, and rests awaits.

The kids are now in bed, I am certain that tonight they will not be misbehaving but sleeping, recovering from today's fatigue. I haven't heard any noise echoing from their room, so I am certain that they are resting. I even excused them from washing the dishes today.

Today was Mokete's day to wash the dishes. He was very happy to hear that he would not be, but there was a debate as to who would be washing them tomorrow.

'Mama, so is Mokete not washing the dishes today, and he is going to wash them tomorrow instead of me? Because I am supposed to wash them tomorrow, or does it mean since his day has passed, I will continue with the timetable as it is tomorrow?

Which I do not think would be fair mama, because we all suffered from today's work.'

Tokelo Hlagala.

This was the youngest's argument, Lesiba. Lesiba is the smartest of my three kids, he reasons like an adult, we have many debates about church and God. Before I could reply to Lesiba, the middle child took her stance.

'Yes mama, what does it mean for tomorrow? I also stand with Lesiba, it cannot be that tomorrow he is the one washing the dishes, and Mokete has gotten away with a free day, we all worked today and are tired, let us have democracy mama'.

By the time I could pass my judgment over the case it was plain clear which party had won the argument.

'Okay, yes Mokete will wash the dishes tomorrow, okay.'

'Ahh mama', this was all Mokete could say to argue his point.

Mokete is not a child of many words, but he is the kindest of all my children. He is from my first failed marriage, a marriage that I walked out of many years ago. It had taken me some time to walk out of that marriage, but the fire had become too intense for me to endure. I had promised myself and my family that I will not let my marriage fail in any manner when I got married. But my in-laws did not like me, the sisters of my then-husband did not like me, and his mother did not like me. I began to suspect that they had been trying to bewitch me because several odd things were happening when I was sleeping.

My then husband worked in the farms as a tractor operator, and he stayed at that particular farm about an hour away. He was usually not home during the week, he only came back on Fridays and left on Mondays. Additionally, to this war that was brewing and going on with my sisters-in-law and mother-in-law, my father-in-law began making moves on me. He would come to my room at night and attempt to sleep with me. One day he took it too far that when I woke up in the morning I packed my bags, took my son who was at the time six years of age, and left.

When I got home that evening my mother scolded me for leaving my in-laws. She told me that in the morning I was to return back. I tried to plead with her by telling her what was going on, how my sisters-in-law and mother-in-law were treating me, but I omitted to say anything about my father-in-law. I did not want to start something I could not finish; I had no evidence, it would be my word against his, a battle I could not win nor did have the energy for.

Tokelo Hlagala.

It was several years later, about five years after that incident that I packed my bags for the last time and went back home. I could no longer withstand the pressure, everyone in that community frowned upon my arrival at weddings, and at funerals. How could I exist in a community where my in-laws had badmouthed me throughout? I could not, so I left.

When I arrived home this time, I was very adamant that I would not return back there no matter what my mother said. I would sleep at her gate if she did not let me in. But on this occasion, she did not even fight me, she was happy to see her grandson. I realized then that she was never the problem, the problem had been my father, he did not want to see his daughter back at home. He came from a generation and culture that believed that no matter the trials, a wife must endure whatever she is put through by her in-laws. There was nothing about my situation he had not heard before, he had said once. This time my father had passed away, part of me was glad he was gone, he had failed to protect me.

Poor Folk/s.

He was never a benevolent father who protected his daughter who appeared to be suffering under the tyranny of her in-laws.
He never really cared for the details of the abuse I was under with my in-laws.
I never really had any relationship with my father, if I was told that he was not my real father I would not be surprised, but I had too much of his resemblance, one did not need a DNA test to figure out he was indeed my father.

I do not recall ever having a conversation about anything with my father throughout my whole life. In all the minute conversations that we had, he was almost always directing me to do something, and I would reply with a yes, never a no. That was the only form of communication we had. He never asked me about my schoolwork when I was young, he never asked me about the man who became my first husband before I married him. In a nutshell, he did not recognize my existence unless there was a chore, he wanted me to render, and yes, as you might predict there was never a thank you from him.

The only affection from a man that I have received, the only man that ever saw me was my first husband. He was kind and generous, perhaps too much, he was a walk over, he never stood his ground regarding how his family treated me, even when I walked away, he did not come for me, he moved on as if nothing happened, and I heard from the grapevine he had another woman in his life. In my perception and estimation, he could never detach from his mother. They say a man shall leave his mother and father to start his own family, I do not think he understood that scripture well even though he was a devoted Christian.

I attributed most of the challenges to his incapacity to detach from his mother, and viewing his father as the authority figure even though he too was a man who had a wife and son. I think if we had not stayed with his family after our marriage, if we had moved out to start our own home, things might not have progressed how they did, there cannot be two men and two women in a single house and things pan out well.

It was a recipe for disaster, but there was little I could do about the situation. I could have not told him we needed to move, he was the breadwinner, one thing that created the animosity between me and my in-laws, part of them felt that I was taking their breadwinner. Being unemployed myself I could not do anything. Women have for a long time not had voices in their marriages because men were and are the breadwinners, it is the narrative of he who feeds you calls the shots, this I have suffered, not only in my first marriage, but in the second one too.

If I was to have another marriage after this one, chances are the same would remain evident.

My father never believed in sending a girl child to school, 'we will send her to school, immediately when she completes and starts working, she will get married and go start a family, what good is that to us, my money would be thrown in the river', my father once said, he was with his friends who all believed the same thing.

What my father said was not foreign in many households in our community, empowering and educating the girl child was seen as a waste of time and money. The role of the girl child is relegated to being a wife to some man, then bearing children for that man, then spending the rest of her life in the tyranny of taking care of the children, cleaning, and rendering catharsis duties to his husband. In the case where the woman can't seem to be able to bear children for her husband, her womanhood title is stripped away. She is no longer seen as a woman, she is discarded by society, and chances are the man is going to leave her, or get a second wife who will bear children for him.

Had I been a boy child my fate would have been different: I would have been empowered in all the ways possible, but many men do not feel they have children until they have a boy child. Maybe this is why my father never saw me, I was a representation of failure in his eyes, I know he wanted a son, he even went to the extreme of trying to have a son outside his marriage. It was well known that he had been disloyal to his wife, but it was not a big deal it turns out. I had always wondered why she never left him, I was bitter for some time, any scintilla of opportunity that remained in me building any relationship with him left after my discovery of his disloyalty. But also, where would she go? I suspect she would not be welcome back at her home, the same way she did not me, when I came back the first time, in addition she did not have a job.

'Yes, I will not stop trying to have a boy child, any man who fails to make a boy child has failed, I refuse to be that man, I now have 4 women that I am visiting daily for this, I am definitely sure one of them will be fruitful', this I overheard once my father talking to our neighbor, I lost respect for both of them. I know of a man who it was speculated died of a heart attack when his wife gave birth to twins on their third attempt, which turned out to be girls, he now had four girls. It is narrated that this is the reason he kicked the bucket.

Five years later after my failed marriage I met my current husband who we have two kids, he on the other hand is not a walk over like my previous, he is stern, tyrannical, no one plays over his head, in fact he does not know any form of play anymore. He used to be a bit kind and caring, but through the vicissitudes of time he became something unrecognizable to me. We hardly have any conversations anymore, he hardly makes any loving and caring gestures, we are hardly intimate anymore. The only time we are is when he wants to catharsis his manly fluid, even this he does without

Tokelo Hlagala.

looking at me, without feeling me, it is almost as if it is a domination action to show me who is the man.

The earth continues to hide itself further from the sun, it is getting darker, the constellations of stars are no longer visible, clouds have covered the atmosphere, rain is near. The growing force of the wind outside is swaying the trees side to side. I can hear the branches rub against the window, the tree by the house will need trimming.

Night goes on living, he still has not returned, like Christians, I am awaiting a man that I have no clue when he will arrive, he has been out all day, this has become his routine, work during the week, spend weekends at the taverns and lord knows where. This has become his life, of what brought about this change in lifestyle I am not aware, but this is how things stand, a fleeting marriage, a wide hole between me and the man that I once shared a life with, now only sharing a house. I used to hear other women complain about how they had become estranged from their husbands, I never knew it could be, and in a few cases, it became evident that these men had mistresses, I think that is the fate that awaits me.

The children are sound asleep, it seems there is no quarreling as to who is sleeping on the floor today. There are two beds in their room, one of the beds sleeps my daughter, the other is supposed to sleep the boys. Some time ago there was an argument that they did not want to sleep together on the same bed, I suspect it is the genesis of puberty in the youngest of the boys. Mokete never had any problems prior. So, they made a timetable like they have one for dishes, they change places every two days. I told them that I did not want to be involved in their sleeping politics when they started.

My exhaustion heightens with each passing second. I need rest, but I sit here hoping he will walk in, I am not certain what time he will arrive, somedays he arrives later than others.

Tokelo Hlagala.

Seated here I am deep in thoughts pondering what might be the cause today, what might be that one thing that sends him off the rails and a pandemonium ensues? I am never certain what causes the pandemonium—the raging thunders I am constantly a recipient of, sometimes they come from the left, sometimes from the right, depending on where I am positioned at the time and where his rage is hammering, on the left side, or on the right side. It used to be slaps only, but it has been taken up a notch, and fists are included, I fear that I may soon graduate, and the slaps and fists are accompanied by an occasional kick in the ribs.

There was a time where he used to apologize, usually, the next day as I would be tending to my wounds, he sometimes would even help, by putting some ice on the swelling, or rubbing some cream, he does that no more. Now it is as if he does not see me, he avoids eye contact, on the few moments that he glances at me his face is cold, his eyes express some semblance of annoyance and anger. There seems to have grown something about me that is an ignition of his animosity and rage, something that when he sees me his blood pressure intensifies.

Poor Folk/s.

I do not know what possesses him, I do not know what changed, but something changed. Maybe it is the pressure he gets from work, but it cannot be, he is good at his work and a lot of people look up to him. I just do not know what happened to him, but in all honesty, I do not care anymore. There was a time where it used to bother me greatly, where I used to stay up in the darkness of the night attempting to understand what is going on. How did we get here? This I carried with me for a long time unaided like Christ carried his cross to his crucifixion.

It is no longer a question of is it going to happen today, but more an inquiry of how it will, what would be the probable cause of this punishment. I sit here wondering and hoping that the kids are asleep and that their eardrums will not absorb the frequency of the noise. I have learned not to make noise, not because I do not feel the pain, but because of them– our children, I do not want them to hear their mother being disempowered, because of the neighbors, I do not want them asking, 'why don't you leave him?' Leave...where would I leave to? Who would I go to? I have started my own family, where would I take these kids of mine? Perhaps if I was without kids I would disappear from the face of the earth and he would never see me, but I cannot, I have a duty, a motherly responsibility to take care of these kids.

The minute one brings children into the world she herself comes second to those children: the well-being of the children is far more essential than hers, she has to ensure that her children are fed before her tastebuds taste anything. These children are too young to be roaming the streets homeless.

These children of mine are what keeps me locked up in this darkness, the darkness that if I decide to leave, there will be unimaginable consequences for them.

So, I seat here wondering, will it be the salty meat? I added just a pinch, bit by bit until I was convinced it was perfect. I had the right amount: I don't think it will be the salt. Will it be the too soft pap? I don't think so, I think it is well balanced, not too soft, and not too hard? Will it be the cold water I bring him to wash his hands with? I will ensure that I test the temperature with my elbow to measure if the condition is right for his hands. Will it be the cold meal? He prefers his food hot, he hates microwaved food, but almost every day he arrives very late after dinner– this is one thing I have no control over, I will just have to cross my fingers on this one, and hope he is in a happy mood.

I can usually hear him from the street as he sings approaching nearer and nearer like an ambulance siren signaling danger, life hanging from a thread, only with this siren the hanging life is mine. I have learned not to waste time and ensure that I unlock the doors as he nears. I have learned not to waste time, that the minute he sits down I quickly bring him water then his food, everything is timed, a few seconds of slip-ups can result in serious repercussions. It is only once I have ensured that he is enjoying the food that I can lock up and go to sleep, tiptoeing with my arm on my chest hoping he does not call me back.

The first time he laid hands on me, it was over the fact that I had locked the door when I went to sleep around 21:30. It was on a Saturday night, and he had gone out to the tavern. I had spent the day doing laundry and was extremely tired, I knew he had his own key so he would not have any problems with coming into the house. But on this occasion, he had left it in the house, a fact that I did not know because he always had it, unknowingly I went to bed. There was a knock on the door. I could hear it was him, I quickly went to open for my husband, he had not even said a single word when he hit me with a thunder of a slap that sent me reeling hitting the chairs and table in the kitchen.

'How did you think I would get into the house when you have locked the doors like this? Do you want me to sleep in the streets when I have a house that I build with my own hands, with my own money?'. This he said to me while I was still holding on to the chair in disbelief, I became dumb and numb for some minutes trying to comprehend what just transpired before my very eyes. My head was spinning, my mind was racing. They say the first one, the first time is always the most memorable and shocking, this moment in my past abides by both the former and latter.

'Give me my damn food woman, don't just stare at me'.
I did not want to agitate him anymore, I quickly gave him food and sat down across from him. I was in a state of momentary trauma, I did not see him seated before me eating, I was lost in the maze of my own shock, traversing my mind

trying to wonder and comprehend what had just happened. I do not know it was after how long when he pushed the plate on the table, and it hit my hands which had been gripping each other, with my mind in wonder, that I realized he was done eating.

He disappeared into the bedroom. I sat there flabbergasted trying to encrypt the chain of events of that night, what had led to this? I went to sleep that night and the days that followed still in shock.

'Did something happen in the tavern? Did someone make him angry', I thought for a while trying to understand. I brushed my cheek tenderly trying to lessen the agony from that gigantic slap I had received from my husband. In the morning I did as I usually did, woke up to warm water on the stove so he could bath before going to work. He had this remorseful face when he woke up, before he took a bath, he grabbed my hand when he found me in the kitchen and apologized, *mother of my children, I am very sorry*. I forgave him and blamed the alcohol.

Tokelo Hlagala.

It was over a month later when something happened again. It was in the early morning of June, I had prepared his bathing water as per usual, and when he went to bath, I returned to sleep.

'Where is my work suite?' he asked after bathing.
'I do not know, where did you put it yesterday'.
I was not asleep, but my eyes were closed when I spoke to him because I was not planning to wake up again. A vicious thunderous slap to my left cheek woke me up, like a drunk man I struggled to compose myself from the stars I was seeing.

'You don't even respect me: you speak to me with your eyes closed. You're the one who organizes everything here, where did you put it?'.
Without a word I stood up in disbelief scanned the room, opened the drawer, and there were his work suites, he had not even bothered to look at the most basic places that even a child could look. He wore his work suites and off he went. I believed he would apologize when he returned, but he did not, he never did and I

was clearly never going to hear, 'I am sorry' from him, he was not even remorseful, from there on the beatings continued one after the other.

Over time his eyes darkened, his face shrunk, the beautiful eyes that had charmed me once upon a time when we first met were no more, the beautiful round face that had swept me off my feet was no more, he became something else.

I am not sure what has happened that has turned him into this monster, his hostility towards me deepens by the day, he is no longer friendly and playful to the kids. They too have stepped away from him, but they do not know the abuse that I endure, I try to conceal it as much as I can. I am glad he does not abuse me in front of the children, but I fear that it is only a matter of time before he does.

I wish there was a way I could escape all this, but where would I escape to? What would I tell my children? How would I support them? There is no escape for me, if only I was much younger, if only I was educated and had employment that would allow me to support my children.

Tokelo Hlagala.

There is a sound outside, someone singing, this is a familiar voice. It is my husband, he is drunk, the clouds are looming, they have begun to let loose drops of water, it is drizzling, the thunders of lighting are near, I can feel them, I am certain.

I have the keys in my hands ready to unlock the door in case he does not have his keys, the food tastes nice and the salt is moderate. I quickly warm some water for his hands.

'Knock, knock'
I run to the door and open, he stands bold before me, I look at him timidly, he looks at me sternly without blinking.

How will it happen?

Poor Folk/s.

Tokelo Hlagala.

My breeders hoped and prayed that "nothing happens" but I happened, and affliction began. Frustrations, fears and feuds fuelled anxieties and they panicked...

A day in the life of Zandi.

'Mam, please pick that up and read it'

If simplicity and predictability were a life, it would be epitomized by the one my mother and I live. There are no radical, adrenaline-influenced activities that we engage in. In fact, there is very little interaction between me and her, between me and the world. I have always been clothed by isolation and solitude. Intimacy is something I enjoy only in the minute moments when I am walking to school with my neighbour. Apart from these moments, I am like a weed growing by the lawn, unseen, unattended.

During weekdays I rise with the morning light and prepare for school. Upon completion, I

94

Poor Folk/s.

knock on Lesley's door. On many occasions, I find Lesley still preparing himself. On some days he opens the door while attempting to wear his shoe, on some days while he is attempting to recollect where his sock is, and on some days still trying to tie his tie. So, many times I must walk into his house and take a seat while he is still lost in his maze of recollections or trying to wear something. It is very clear that Lesley is clumsy, or perhaps he just has a lot going on in his life. Most of the mornings Aus Thandi, Lesley's mother would already have left for work when I come knocking.

Two things are most likely when I return home from school in the afternoons, I will find my mother either sleeping or with one of her many male friends. The reason she many times sleeps during the day is that she works during the night.

At around 18:00 on weekdays, my mother usually leaves home. She is always well dressed, a knee-high dress, make-up, and her tiny side bag. She is really beautiful when she goes to work. I someday wish to be as pretty as she is when I find a job, although I do not envy working during the night, I already struggle with waking up in the morning in winter, imagine working the whole night in winter, it would be unbearable I imagine.

Between Monday and Thursday, mother usually works from 18:00 to 23:00 roughly speaking. On Fridays she sometimes works and arrives the next morning. A few of the other ladies here like my mother work during the night, I sometimes see them in the morning when I am going to school, and they are just coming in. I am not sure as to whether they work at the same place as my mother or a different place, but like my mother, they too look very pretty. All of them are kind, they always smile and wave at me, and I wave back with a gesture of a smile too.

When I was much younger, two years ago, my mother used to leave me with Aus Thandi and Lesley. It was during this period that I began to develop a strong familial bond with both Lesley and Aus'Thandi, they became the family I never had. Lesley became a brother to me, a friend to me, when I heard him say, *'If anyone tries to give you trouble, you tell me, I will deal with them accordingly'*, that was a confirmation that he saw me as his little sister. I used to believe that there were no forces that could destruct the bond I have with him. But recently he has found a girlfriend, one of his classmates, we now walk together, the three of us, she stays two blocks from us.

Lesley's girlfriend is very pretty, last year she won the beauty pageant competition at school since then she has gained status and fame. She was not always known, and that is because she previously attended a different school and only came to ours this year. She is already a valedictorian, I like her a lot, but at the same time, I lowkey hate her and envy her. I was never aware that hate and love could coexist till I met her, I thought we either loved people or hated them, not both.

I like her because she is a nice person and does not make fun of me, but at the same time, I hate her because she is nice, and people like her. I am nice, but no one likes me, not even my mother, and I get a distinct feeling that Lesley likes her more than he likes me.

I see it in his eyes, how he looks at her, how they play together, it is so beautiful, he never plays with me akin to her, he does not look at me akin to her, one might even say his gaze towards me is of pity, pity for the girl who no one likes, but that might just be my mind playing tricks on me.

Tokelo Hlagala.

I have this revolting feeling that she will take Lesley away from me soon, or someday, that it is only a matter of time, right now she is still planning her heist, she wants Lesley to like her, she wants me to like her, that is why she is nice to me. But when the right moment comes, she will strike like lightning, leaving behind a mass of destruction and tremors, and pain in others–me.

Oh! Lesley, the only person that likes me and takes care of me, who will like me and take care of me when Lesley now focuses his time solely on his girlfriend and forgets about my meagre insignificant existence?

Will I even have anyone to walk with to school? Who will punish my mockers and tormentors now that my knight is ebbing into the hands of another woman? Is this how it feels to lose a man? I know my loss is inevitable. In a couple of months, my predicament will ensue, both Lesley and his girlfriend are currently in grade 7, which means in the coming year they will be transitioning to high school, and I will still have two more years to go in primary.

I have heard them talk about their future, about next year, how they both want to go to the same school so they can spend quality time together. I know sadly that, by the time I get to high school her mission would be complete, there will be nothing I can do, there will be no more space for me in Lesley's life, my benevolent brother and neighbour would be a gone boy.

How I wish Lesley would fail his current grade, that would give me one more year with him, that would mean our walks to and back from school would not be perturbed by her, and she probably wouldn't want to be with someone who has failed. She would go on to find someone else at her high school, Lesley will be heartbroken, I will be there for him as a little sister to nurse his wounds. I believe that our bond will grow stronger, the fire will continue to burn, warming my existence, bestowing me light and energy.

I really envy Lesley's girlfriend, I wish I could win the pageant, I wish I had her strong persona and confidence, I wish people liked me at school like they do her, and I am very sure her mother also likes her. I am sure she gives her attention, unlike mine, if only wishes where horses, only then would a beggar like myself ride.

Tokelo Hlagala.

It used to be around 22:30 when my mother would fetch me from Lesley's. She would usually carry me because I would be asleep by then. She would carry me because she did not want to wake me. In all honesty, I mostly heard her when she would pick me up, I would wake but not open my eyes, which would have meant that I would not get my lift for the day and I would have to walk on my own, I did not want to miss out on that fun. But I get the feeling that my mother knew I was not sleeping, that she too enjoyed carrying me, that is perhaps one of the few intimate and fond moments that we had together. Those were the occasions that I felt very close to my mother, both emotionally and physically. But now that routine is no more, ever since I got to grade five, she has said to me that I am now old enough to look after myself and not burn down the house.

Before my mother leaves, she ensures that she has prepared food for me and all I have to do is eat and wash my dish. Her instructions are that I should sleep by 20:00 or there will be trouble, she told me that Aus Thandi was her spy, and she would tell her if she heard the tv play after 20:01. On days where I really want to watch tv and it is past 20:00, I play the tv with the volume extremely low, I sit right an inch away from the tv so I can be the only one that hears it.

Whenever I see other learners dropped off and picked up at school by their fathers, I become sad, wishing that I at least knew my father, even if he did not drop me off at school, but the mere feeling and security of having a father, knowing him even if he did not stay with me.

Of my father, I know very little. I have never met my biological father, I do not know whether he is still alive, or if he passed on, if he is staying near to where we stay, or in some faraway lands, if he knows of my existence or he does not, if he is alone somewhere with no kids, or if he has a family, a wife, and kids. I have wondered before if I have any of his traits, like my penchants for self-monologues, does he also have a tendency to speak with himself? Is he like me without friends? Do people like him? I am short in stature, I wonder if I inherited that from him, or if it was merely genetic luck, since my mother is tall. I wonder if my cursive handwriting comes from him because it sure as hell does not come from my mother. The one thing that I am certain of as pertaining to my characteristics is that I inherited my eyebrows and big eyes from my mother. My mother has the most beautiful glowing eyes I have ever seen.

The closest I have had to a father was through a figure called Samson. Samson is the first man that I came to know from the moment I could understand what a man was, I must have been three years of age or so. He was someone that looking back now I could label as my mother's boyfriend. Samson used to come to our place a lot, sometimes he slept over. We did visit his place too, but not even once did we sleep over. He used to buy us groceries, he used to buy me sweets and gifts, so I had a liking to him, but somehow, I never called him father, my mother had never told me to call him father, and he too never requested that from me. Come to think of it, I never referred to him as anything, no title, but I knew his name was Samson because that is what my mother used to call him.

Samson was in my life for two years, and someday he just stopped coming by, and we stopped going to him. I never knew what happened to him, I have always wondered, and continue to wonder, where is he? what happened to him? Who did he become?

From that period on there was an endless pouring of men at our flat, many of them did not talk to me. I got a feeling that perhaps they were not allowed to speak to me or share any pleasantries with me. Most of them just looked at me and offered me a forced smile before they disappeared into my mother's bedroom or wherever they came from. Mother appears to be a bubbly and joyous person with these male friends of hers, but the minute they step out it is as though her light and glow darken, as if the glow that was once expressed and illuminated on her face was a pleasure indulging façade primarily for these friends of hers.

I spend most of my days and nights at home alone. I used to spend my days after school with Lesley, but those moments slowly have ebbed my fears were not misplaced evidently, he now mostly spends his time with his girlfriend, but we still walk together to school in the morning and after school.

I wish so much to be like my mother, so I can have a lot of friends like her, so I can have people that I play with like she does in her

Tokelo Hlagala.

room with her friends, they sometimes make noise when they are playing, sometimes they play the tv loudly as they play, so I do not hear their sounds and screams. I think maybe the reason my mother has so many friends is because she is pretty, I know people like pretty people, I can see it at school with Lerato in addition to my mother and Lesley's girlfriend.

Everyone loves Lerato, the boys at our school crawl at her feet, and give her attention, the other girls at school want to be her friend, and she is also the teacher's favourite. Whenever the teachers want something from the staff room they choose her for the task, whenever they want someone to write down the noisemakers, they choose her. This year they have chosen her as the class rep together with Tomas.

I spent a lot of days praying to God that he should bless me with friends, but he has not. I soon realized that people only want to be friends with people who are pretty, and with people who are light skinned. I know this because both my mother, Lesley's girlfriend, and Lerato are light-skinned and pretty, and they are liked by everyone. And so, I have stopped praying for friends but for prettiness

Poor Folk/s.

and lighter skin, inevitably I know friends will follow.

After Samson disappeared, there came another man into our life, his name was Lesiba. Lesiba drove some sort of bakkie, the difference between the relationship we had with him is that me and my mother never visited him, but he visited us, in actual fact he visited my mother because he never spoke to me. His arrival time was usually around 19:00, it would be around 21:00 when he left, I would hear as the burglar was shut that he had left. On nights that Lesiba came, I think it is the days that mother was on her day-offs because she did not go to work at all on those days. Lesiba kept on coming for some weeks but soon disappeared. I did not even notice his disappearance because he had never spoken to me, he had never seen me, he acted like I was non-existent when he came and slid quickly into my mother's room like a stone vacating a slingshot. I felt that he had some arrogance, from the way he walked and his facial expression, I could tell he was not a pleasant person. When I came to realize that he was no longer coming I said 'good riddance' to myself, my mother could surely get a better friend.

The man that followed after Lesiba was a man that I never got to know by name. This gentleman had a polite face with his potbelly and *chiskop*. He looked like someone who had money, I never got to see the car that he drove only heard its beastly groaning engine as it left our place in the late evenings, but he did not last.

After him began a period of an endless chain of men one after the other, and oddly they seem to be once-off friends. They hardly return, I am not certain if my mother has developed a no return policy. It was around this period that mother began going to work less, she mentioned that she would now spend the most time working from home, only leaving for work on Fridays and the weekend.

Out of all the men that have come into our life, my all-time favourite is my mother's current friend, he is the kindest man that I have ever come across. His name is *Moshe*, this he told me himself, after almost a year of not having any of my mother's friends talk to me, he

Poor Folk/s.

talked to me, he saw me, I was finally a person, something that aroused interest, something that deserved to be asked, '*how are you?*'.

I recall vividly the first day he came into our house, it was a day just after Valentine. It was a Friday evening around 18:00 when he knocked at the door. '*I wonder who that is because Aus Thandi is at work*', this my mother said before she stood and approached the door. I was not permitted to ever open the door when there was a knock unless it was Aus Thandi or Lesley, and they too knew to announce who they were when knocking, and I knew their voices which made it simple, but any knocks apart from theirs, I did not approach the door. I would listen as the knocker slowly lost gusto, then their footsteps would retreat and recede slowly from the door down the hallway, and I would resume whatever I was up to. I would not even tell my mother later on that there was someone here, she never asked, and I doubted that she cared.

'*You're an hour early, you should not be here before 19:00*', my mother said to the person I could not see because the door was slightly ajar, not fully open for me to see whoever was on the other side.

'Oh, yea we knocked off early today, so I figured why wait'.

'Okay come on inside, take a seat there as I quickly freshen up'.
This stranger walked in leaving my mother to close the door behind him. He sat on the nearest couch from the door, it was the uncomfortable couch, one could feel the planks beneath the worn-out leather and sponges that were covering the couch. I wanted to highlight to him that the couch he selected was the least comfortable, but by now I had learned to mind my business.

My mother had already disappeared into the bathroom to freshen up. This stranger was now in my company, in my little world of isolation.

'Mickey mouse is my niece's favourite, we used to watch it together,' he said to me glancing at the television screen.

I wasn't expecting him to talk to me since he had not greeted me, but I was not offended because no one ever did, but I was shocked.

That is when he caught my attention and I looked towards his direction, I was seated on a mat on the floor, with my back against the other couch directly opposite the television, somehow, I prefer sitting down when watching television. I was stunned and simultaneously excited by his remarks.

'Oh really, you watch Micky mouse? he is my favourite too, although I have no one to watch him with, do you stay with your niece?' I inquired to this new friend of mom, who I might just expropriate.

'Yes, I love him a lot, including Spongebob, also Jake and the neverland pirates, but I am sure you watch them once a while with your mother'

'Oh wow, I love those too, nah I never watch them with my mother, in fact, I never do anything with my mother, she is always busy at work or sleeping recovering from work'

'Your niece, do you stay with him?' I asked again thinking he might have not heard me initially.

'No, I used to, she passed away three years ago, now I no longer watch them because they would just make me miss her excessively, I loved her really, she was the centre of my life, she was a very bubbly child, she never stopped making trouble, but I loved her nonetheless'.

'Oh, I am sorry to hear that about your niece, I don't know how it feels like to lose someone you love. I have never lost anyone in that manner, in fact, I have never lost anyone because I never really have had anyone, maybe Lesley, but we still walk to school together even though we no longer play together because of his new girlfriend, but I don't think that counts, it is very minor as compared to yours, but from what you're saying, it must be painful. I also wonder if I died today would there be anyone who feels about my death like you feel about your niece, would anyone stop watching Mickey mouse because it reminds them of me? Because they feel sad by watching it? I doubt anyone would feel about me the way you feel about your niece'.

'It is okay, she is with God, I go to see her grave whenever I miss her.'

'Yes, my teacher told me that when people die, they go to God in heaven, what is your name Mr.?'

Poor Folk/s.

'My name is Jonah, but you can call me Bhut Jo'

'Okay Bhut Jo, are you like the Jonah in the bible? At school during bible lessons, they once told us about a guy who was also Jonah, I think he was swallowed by a fish or shark because he did not listen to God, I don't recall the story, I was not really paying attention to the teacher, I have a complicated relationship with God...'

'... you know my mother's friends never speak to me: you seem like a kind person. I never have anyone to speak to, Lesley used to be the one I spent time with, but since he has a girlfriend, we hardly speak, and the other kids at school don't talk to me at all, I wish I was pretty like Mom and Lerato so people could speak to me and like me, and I could have friends like you are my mom's friend.'

'Ha-ha! I know about that Jonah, luckily God has not sent me anywhere so far. Who is Lesley and who is Lerato?'

'Lesley is the boy from next door that I walk with to school, Lerato is the pretty light-skinned girl in our class who is loved by everyone.'

Tokelo Hlagala.

'Oh, I see, you are very pretty believe me'

'If you were not old, I would accusingly say you are lying to me. But I know I am not pretty, I am not, other people don't think what you are saying now, they don't think I am pretty, if I was, they would like me and talk to me.'

'Do old people lie?'

'I don't think so.'

'So, I can't be lying to you when I say you are pretty, and I promise to talk to you every day that I come here to prove to you that you are.'

'Okay Bhut' Jo, we will see.'

We were still engaged in a pleasant conversation when my mother called Bhut Jo, and they disappeared into her room.

I was happy that for once someone saw me and talked to me, and actually liked me and said I was pretty. I went to sleep that day very happy and hoped that my mother would stay friends with Bhut Jo forever because he was unlike the other friends she had, he was nice.

Bhut'Jo has become a regular at our house, he used to come at least two days a week, then he started sleeping over, I knew then that he and mother were boyfriend and girlfriend, although I am not fully sure. Whenever Bhut Jo visits he brings me nice things, snacks, and sweets and he talks to me a bit before he disappears with mother into her room.

Bhut' Jo now comes to my room and plays with me at night when mother is sleeping, he says that we must use the time wisely because during the day mother takes all the time with him. We play games that I have never played with anyone, they mostly involve us taking off our clothes and him entering inside of me. The first time we played this game I felt painful inside of me when we were playing and the next day as I went to school. But Bhut Jo told me that even mother used to feel the pain when they were playing, and she got used to it, and I too will get used to it, and he was right, I now no longer feel the pain as I used to. Most of the times I do not know how to play, but he shows me what to do.

I am happy that I now have someone to play with, even though we mostly play during the night when mother is sleeping.'

Tokelo Hlagala.

'What is this I just read? Zandi's mother asked in wonder.

'Mam, this is the homework your child was given by her English teacher...she told them to paint a picture of their daily lives'. The police officer spoke looking sternly at her together with the social worker.

Poor Folk/s.

Tokelo Hlagala.

Acknowledgements.

Tis book would have not seen the light of day without a variety of people who each played a significant role throughout the journey of preparing this meal.

Howard Zondo and Phumulani Mngomezulu, we have spent countless hours discussing the book and how to illuminate the human condition, your thoughts and feedback have been greatly essential in the making of this book.

Phumuzile Mahlangu, Zuko Gqadavama, Zizipho Ludidi, I am grateful for your dedication, to the editing and proofreading of this book throughout, it has become finer and finer through your suggestions.

Masego Shotholo, for your support in the very early stages of this book. Ofentse Letsoalo, Ducks Dammans, for the continued support in my business endeavors. KCS members (Kagiso Molefe, Sharon Sindane, Sakhile Ngobe, Lethabo

Poor Folk/s.

Mohlatlole, Mogau Setsiba, Busi Nobeleza and Otlotleng Monyoko), all the sessions we have had hitherto, have contributed to this book in a lot of ways.

Toni Simanga, to the many times we have sat discussing books, engaged in philosophical discourses, to the many books you have bestowed me, I am grateful.

Orapeleng Simanga, I am grateful for our relationship and the great effort that was placed in preparation of the artwork for the book cover. I could have not chosen a better artist to illuminate the ideas I had.

Aubrey Nkanyani, for the beautiful work you have done with the book cover, I am grateful.

To my siblings, for the support, especially all the money I took from you in the process of making this book.

To mom and dad, this book would not be possible without having a home, a comfortable place to allow me the creative process away from the many cares, worries and the demands of life.

Tokelo Hlagala.

Both of you were the final proofreaders of this book and showed me what needed to be fixed, I am eternally grateful for your support and feedback

Sello Mokonyama, to the many times you called me asking when am I writing a book, your endless calls have been significant.

Kutloano Malahlela, for the many times you asked me when am I writing a book, and for being the first buyer of the book even before it was printed, I am grateful.

To the many literary figures that I have worked with, the many that trusted me with their manuscripts when I was starting this journey with little experience, through our interactions I have learned.

To my English teacher Mr. Ntsoane, you first saw my writing potential those many years ago when you challenged me to prove to you that I could write a better essay than the previous.

To the many learners that have been part of our storytelling and writing workshops, your continuous questions have forced me to deepen my inquiry into the many cubicles of storytelling and writing.

Lastly, I am grateful to the many life experiences, especially the somber ones, without them this book might not be in existence.

Asante.

About the author.

Tokelo Hlagala is a student of the
HUMAN CONDITION.